This book
belongs to

_____

_____

Little Grey Rabbit

AND FRIENDS

Little Grey Rabbit

AND FRIENDS

By Alison Uttley
Pictures by Margaret Tempest

templar publishing

Contents

Little Grey Rabbit and Friends

Alison Uttley published her first Little Grey Rabbit book in 1929. Based on a brilliantly imagined community of animals with homely, sensible Little Grey Rabbit, vain and selfish Squirrel and the boastful and adventurous Hare at their centre, these little books, beautifully and sensitively illustrated by Margaret Tempest, were soon selling in their hundreds of thousands, making their author, Alison Uttley, a household name.

Alison Uttley was convinced that children loved the Little Grey Rabbit characters 'because I believe in them. Mine aren't made up, they're real…I was born in a place of beauty…I talked to all the animals'. Brought up as the unusually gifted daughter of a tenant farmer and his wife in the hilly Derbyshire countryside, Alison was indeed surrounded by animals on her beloved and remote Castle Top Farm and those in the surrounding woods and fields. She felt that animals 'have such a raw deal, and I think they are very faithful and very, very patient.'

She wrote 'In these little books I always try to give some specially English touch of country life, which might [otherwise] be forgotten.' More than this, she imbued her characters with qualities that can be seen as quintessentially English. This is made clear in this latest collection of tales where, apart from the central triumvirate of Little Grey Rabbit, Squirrel and Hare, four more of her best-known and strongest characters have their stories told and their personalities and foibles explored.

There is Moldy Warp the mole, taciturn, level headed, practical and helpful, sometimes digging up valuable old Roman gold coins, sometimes damping down Hare's wilder fantasies. Then there is the Speckledy Hen, fussily maternal; always clucking over her brood of chicks, somewhat scatty, fond of a gossip and inclined to noisy panic if she fears the fox is prowling. Wise Owl is aloof and often patronising, though mostly willing to give advice and even to hand out instructive books from his library in the hollow tree, but also a slightly menacing presence as he glides overhead on silent wings. Finally there is the skulking Rat, in whose tail Squirrel ties a knot to stop his habitual thieving, even though he is chiefly trying to feed his hungry family; this story though has a redemptive ending when Rat discovers he has the skill to carve beautiful and useful objects with his sharp teeth and thus need not steal to survive.

What a treat awaits those readers that are meeting these enchanting, occasionally infuriating, but always fascinating and believable characters for the first time.

Denis Judd
London
2016

The latest edition of Professor Denis Judd's authorised biography, Alison Uttley: Spinner of Tales *was published in 2010; he is also editor of her Diaries,* The Private Diaries of Alison Uttley, 1932–1971, *paperback 2011*

Foreword
by Alison Uttley

Of course you must understand that Grey Rabbit's home had no electric light or gas, and even the candles were made from pith of rushes dipped in wax from the wild bees' nests, which Squirrel found. Water there was in plenty, but it did not come from a tap. It flowed from a spring outside, which rose up from the ground and went to a brook. Grey Rabbit cooked on a fire, but it was a wood fire, there was no coal in that part of the country. Tea did not come from India, but from a little herb known very well to country people, who once dried it and used it in their cottage homes. Bread was baked from wheat ears, ground fine, and Hare and Grey Rabbit gleaned in the cornfields to get the wheat.

The doormats were plaited rushes, like country-made mats, and cushions were stuffed with wool gathered from the hedges where sheep pushed through the thorns. As for the looking-glass, Grey Rabbit found the glass, dropped from a lady's handbag, and Mole made a frame for it. Usually the animals gazed at themselves in the still pools as so many country children have done. The country ways of Grey Rabbit were the country ways known to the author.

A.U.

Moldy Warp
the Mole

Moldy Warp sat in his armchair one morning, examining a tiny square stone. It was painted with a golden eye which seemed to watch the Mole wherever he went. It looked at him when he cooked his mushroom breakfast, when he made his hard little bed, and when he polished his pennies.

"Where this came from there will be the rest of the picture," he thought. "There are only two creatures who could tell me about it. One is Wise Owl, who is asleep by day and fierce by night. The other is Brock the Badger, and where he lives nobody knows."

Moldy Warp washed the small stone in the stream which conveniently ran along the floor of his room, and he rubbed it on his sleeve.

"Now this is an eye of long ago," said Mole to himself.
"It belonged to somebody's picture book – a stone picture book.
I've not found any treasure since I made Owl's bell. I'll go to
Hearthstone Pasture and see if I can find anything more of it."

He took his bright spade from the corner, and brushed his
hair and whiskers. Then he went round his house to lock all
the back doors. There were thirteen of them, each leading to a
different molehill.

Mole went down the passage to the front door. This led him
out near the holly tree. He cut a short stick and started up the
fields with the spade and a bag on his back.

He hadn't gone far when he saw an animal leaping across the field, trying to catch his slender shadow.

"Hallo, Hare!" cried the Mole. "What's the matter?"

"I'm a Mad March Hare!" shouted Hare. "I'm always like this when the March wind blows. I can't help it."

"But it's the month of May," objected Mole.

"It may be May! But there's a March wind, forgotten by somebody, blowing in this field. Where are you going with that spade and sack, Moldy Warp?"

Mole hesitated. He didn't really want Hare's company. Then his good temper overcame him.

"I'm going treasure hunting," said he.

"Oh Moldy Warp! Can I go with you?" Hare quivered with excitement.

"Yes," sighed Mole.

"I'll run ahead and save your short legs, Moldy," said Hare, and he galloped off and was soon out of sight. Mole plodded slowly on his way.

In the next field a little figure stooped here and there, and Mole recognised Little Grey Rabbit.

"Cuckoo!" he called. The rabbit ran with a glad cry to meet him.

"I was gathering cowslips to make a cowslip ball," said she. "Where are you going, Moldy Warp?"

"I'm going on a treasure hunt," replied Mole.

"Can I come with you?" she asked. Then she stopped. "It isn't like a fox hunt is it?"

"Not at all," said Mole. "It's like the hunt the thimble, deep down in the ground."

She walked by his side, talking of cowslip balls and cherry pie and fox's gloves. Every now and then she stopped to gather another cowslip. Mole went solemnly on, and, with a light scutter of feet she caught him up.

Then Squirrel came bounding from a nut tree.

"Hallo! Where are you two going?"

"Treasure hunting," said Grey Rabbit happily. "Come along Squirrel and help to carry it."

"I'm not dressed for treasure hunting," said Squirrel, and she stooped over a pool and stuck a cowslip in her dress. "I ought to have put on my new ribbon."

Then she scampered after Grey Rabbit, and walked by her side, eagerly whispering to her.

Shrill laugher and cries came from over a wall, and there, playing in the cornfield was a crowd of small rabbits.

They came scampering up to the Mole as he crawled through a hole in the wall. "Please, Sir, what time is it?" they asked.

Before Mole could look at the sun, Grey Rabbit replied, "Half-past kissing time, and time to kiss again."

All the little rabbits rubbed their noses, and trotted after Little Grey Rabbit.

"Where is Mole going?" they whispered.

"Sh-sh-sh," Grey Rabbit lowered her voice. "He's going treasure hunting."

Mole led them through a shady lane along little paths that only animals know.

Then the procession passed through a field. Out of the thick grass came Hedgehog with two pails of milk.

"Hallo! Moldy Warp, and Little Grey Rabbit and Squirrel, and all of you little 'uns! Where are you going so fast this morning?" he asked.

"Treasure hunting," replied Mole.

"I'll go along with you," said Hedgehog. "Come here, Fuzzypeg," he called. The shy little fellow came out of the grass with a butterfly net. "Come treasure hunting. You can help to catch it if it flies away."

Soon they were joined by the Speckledy Hen and some fieldmice, all eager to hunt.

"There's rather a crowd," sighed Moldy Warp. "I shall be glad to get underground."

At last they got to Hearthstone Pasture, where dark rocks lay on the smooth grass like black sheep.

"This is where I found my little square stone," Mole told them. "It was underneath the old hawthorn tree. Now wait while I go down and hunt for the treasure."

The animals sat round the tree and watched him. He took his sharp spade and began to dig. Then he seized his sack and wriggled down into the earth out of sight.

"Let's have a treasure hunt, too," cried Squirrel. "And Grey Rabbit shall give a prize."

So they all ran about the field peering among the rocks, poking their noses into crannies, sniffing and seeking.

One rabbit found a jay's feather, and another a wren's nest. Some found flowers and ladybirds, and one found a silk bag full of spider's eggs.

"Look what I've found," called Squirrel, and she pointed to Hare, fast asleep under a rock.

"Where's the treasure?" he cried, rubbing his eyes.

"The prize is won by Fuzzypeg," announced Little Grey Rabbit, and she showed his find. It was a four-leafed clover.

"What is the prize?" asked Hare.

"The cowslip ball," said Grey Rabbit, who had been industriously threading the cowslip on a grass. She gave the yellow flowery ball to Fuzzypeg, who tossed it up in the air and caught it.

"The young rabbits ought to go home," said Grey Rabbit, "and Fuzzypeg. It's getting late."

"Oh no! Let us stay up tonight," they implored.

"We can't desert old Mole," said Fuzzypeg.

"Let us call him," suggested Little Grey Rabbit.

So they all put their paws to their mouths and gave the hide-and-seek cry, "Cuckoo. Cherry tree. Moldy Warp, you can't see me."

A blue veil of darkness slowly covered the fields. The rabbits clustered round Grey Rabbit and the youngest one clung to her skirt.

"I'm cold," he whimpered.

"Let us make a tent and all get inside," said Grey Rabbit.

Squirrel gathered long pointed leaves from a chestnut tree, and Hare stood on tiptoe to pull branches of flowery May.

The little fieldmice took their needles and cottons from their pockets, and sewed the leaves with tiny stitches, white and small as their own teeth.

Grey Rabbit pinned the strips together with thorn pins, and Hedgehog fixed a tent pole in the ground. Soon there was a fine leafy tent, sprinkled with hawthorn blossoms and prickly with thorns, standing in the field.

They all crept into the tent and cuddled together. Little Grey Rabbit told them the story of a white rabbit named Cinderella, who went to a ball, and lost her glass slipper.

The little animals closed their eyes and fell asleep.

"Snuff! Sniff! I smell Rabbit," muttered a Fox.

He glided round the little tent. "Here's a little green bush where no tree used to be." He put his nose close to the leaves and opened his mouth.

"I'll puff and I'll huff and I'll blow their little house down," he muttered. But the prickles of Old Hedgehog stuck in his chin, and the spikes of little Fuzzypeg scratched his nose, and all the thorns of the tent ran into his skin.

"It's a trap," grumbled the Fox, and he ran off.

Now all this time Mole was underground. He went along smooth winding paths, up steps and down, through a little door and into a room.

On the floor stood a stone crock filled with gold.

"Am I dreaming?" he asked himself.

Footsteps padded near, and a large Badger entered the room. "Moldy Warp! How did you get here? I've never had a visitor in all my life!" exclaimed the Badger.

He lighted a lantern and Mole blinked his dim eyes with amazement. On the floor was a picture of a blue and green dolphin. It was made of bright little square stones, but one tiny stone was missing. The lovely dolphin had only one eye.

Mole brought out his little stone. It exactly fitted, like a square in a puzzle.

"The missing eye, lost for many years!" cried Badger excitedly. "Thank you! Only a wise Mole could have found the ancient Dolphin's eye."

The Badger held up his lantern to a cupboard in the wall and showed Moldy Warp his treasures. On the shelves were tiny figures, all carved out of coloured stones, gold necklaces and glass beads.

"How beautiful they are!" cried Mole.

"You shall have a few to take to your own house, Moldy Warp," replied Badger.

Mole modestly chose a little grey stone rabbit, but the Badger lifted down little animals of jade and amber and dropped them into Mole's sack.

"They will do for doorsteps for your fourteen doors, Moldy Warp," said he. "And here's the crock of gold."

Mole thanked him, and shook his great paw.

"Come and have some supper," said the Badger.

He drew a jug of heather ale, and cut a hunch of sweet herb bread and some slices of cold ham. Then by the light of the lantern, the two ate and drank.

"Your health, Badger," said Mole, sipping heather ale. "My! This is good!"

"Made from a long-forgotten recipe," said the Badger. "I'll give you a pitcher of it to carry home."

Then the Badger talked of days of long ago, when the Romans came to England and made the stone picture floors, such as Mole had seen.

As he talked, Mole's eyes began to close, his head nodded, and he dropped off to sleep.

When he awoke he lay in a truckle bed, tucked up with linen sheets. He looked around for Badger, but the great animal had gone. Mole picked up his bag and crock, put the spade on his shoulder, and clasped the jug of heather ale.

He wandered along the confusing maze of passages, until at last he found himself in the open field.

He trotted as fast as he could to the hawthorn tree, calling, "Coo-oo. Coo-oo!"

Hedgehog put his head through the tent opening and saw Mole.

"Here he is! Here's lost Moldy Warp!" he shouted, and the rest came tumbling after him into the field.

"Have you found the treasure, Moldy Warp?" they cried excitedly. Mole opened his sack and emptied out the little cocks, the jade hedgehogs, the amber rabbits and a squirrel of green bronze.

"Oh my!" cried the little rabbits and fieldmice.

"Where did you find these?" asked Grey Rabbit.

Mole shook his head. "It's a secret that can never be told," he said.

Then all the animals insisted on helping carry Mole's treasure. Each one took a precious little toy and galloped off down the fields.

"Be careful!" he called. But they ran faster than ever, eager to get home.

Some dropped their treasure in the long grass, and some lost them in the hedgerows. The fieldmice threw theirs away because they were too heavy. Hedgehog left his jade hedgehog in the cowshed, and the cow ate it with her hay.

Hare leapt over a gorse bush and the amber hare fell from his pocket. Squirrel put her bronze squirrel on a wall and forgot about it.

Little Grey Rabbit carried the pitcher of heather ale without spilling a drop. She left it at Mole's front door, and hurried home to cook breakfast for Squirrel and Hare.

"Ah me!' sighed the Mole, when he arrived hours later. "I'm glad I carried my crock of gold myself."

He waddled slowly into his pantry with the heather ale.
"That's safe, thanks to Grey Rabbit," said he.
He polished the gold coins on his fur sleeve till they shone and looked admiringly at the pictures of eagles and lions engraved upon them.

There was a rat-tat-tat at the door and he went to open it.

"They are all very sorry they lost your treasures, Moldy Warp," said Little Grey Rabbit, stepping in with the Old Hedgehog's milk pail full of flowers. "They have sent you these instead."

She filled a jug with silver daisies and golden buttercups.

"You like them just as much, don't you, Moldy Warp?" she asked wistfully.

"More, much more," answered the Mole. "What is a precious stone to a living flower?"

Yet he gave a deep sigh.

He put his hand in his pocket and brought out his forgotten little stone rabbit. He put it in the middle of the mantelpiece and Grey Rabbit stood on tiptoes to look at it.

"I'm going to give a picnic to all the animals who kindly waited for me in that cold wild pasture up there on the hill," said Mole. "Please ask them to come tomorrow afternoon, Grey Rabbit."

Little Grey Rabbit ran to spread the good news.

The next day they all appeared, dressed in their best clothes. There was Mole ready for them, with the tablecloth spread out on the daisies and the jug of flowers in the middle.

He had provided wild raspberries, rosepetal jam, bluebell jelly, lettuces and tiny red carrots.

"Your very good health, Moldy Warp," called Hare, as he sipped the sun-filled honey ale which filled the tiny glasses.

"Good health! Good luck!" cried the others.

Mole nodded and smiled and sat back with his velvet coat glossy in the sunshine. What a lot of good friends he had, to be sure!

The
Speckledy Hen

ONE MORNING IN SPRING, when the primroses and cowslips were out in the fields, and the violets were blue under the hedges, the Speckledy Hen took a walk. She had decided to leave the farmyard with all its noisy company and live alone.

Robins, blackbirds, thrushes, fieldmice, and rabbits looked at her and shook their heads when she asked if there was room for her. So she left that field and tripped lightly across a narrow wood to a pasture, where a stream ran. In an oak tree was a round hole. The Speckledy Hen had seen it once, but somebody was living there.

The Speckledy Hen found the oak tree, and she walked round it, clucking softly. Nobody was there. She entered quietly.

Yes, it was a nice comfortable room, just the right size for a nursery.

She went to the field and picked a bunch of broom twigs. She twisted them into a little brush and carried it to the house. She swept out the dead leaves and brushed the walls. She tossed the little old bed out of the door, and threw away a musty blanket. Then she shooed out a fat spider, a family of earwigs and a beetle.

"Away with you," she cried. "I don't want any webs in my nice house."

When all was tidy the Speckledy Hen hunted for some nice dry moss, and she covered the floor with the carpet.

Satisfied with her morning's work, she went back to the farm and climbed the stair to the hen-house. She got together a bundle of her belongings, and stuffed a few things under her feathery wings. Then, looking extremely fat, she waddled across the farmyard and out of the gate.

"Where are you going, dear Speckledy?" asked the Cock.

"That's a secret," said she, and the Cock laughed and crowed, "Cock-a-doodle Doo."

He was used to the Speckledy Hen's secrets. She always was a Hen who liked her own way.

"Your bonnet's crooked," said he.

The Speckledy Hen couldn't straighten her bonnet because her wings were hiding a frying-pan, a sack of meal, a bag of Indy corn, some little loaves and a teapot.

"I'll put it right my dear," said the Cock, and gave it a tilt over her eye.

"There. That's better. You look very smart for visiting, my love." He threw her a kiss, but the Speckledy Hen said nothing. She marched off into the field.

"Hallo!" said the Hare. "Where are you off to, looking so handsome and fat, Speckledy Hen?"

"Off to make a secret," said she.

"Mind you don't meet the Fox," said Hare.

Further on she met Fuzzypeg, dawdling across the field, swinging his schoolbag.

"Good-day, Speckledy Hen," said Fuzzypeg. "Can I carry anything for you?"

"No, thank you, Fuzzypeg," puffed the Hen. "Have you been a good urchin, and done your lessons well?"

"Yes. I'm learning to read now," said the little hedgehog proudly. "I can read long words like Treacle and Barley-sugar."

"There's Barley-sugar in my pocket, if you can find it," said the Speckledy Hen.

Fuzzypeg stuck a little fist among her feathers and brought out a yellow stick.

The Speckledy Hen walked as fast as she could to the hollow oak tree. She panted through the little doorway and dropped all her parcels on the floor. She was so weary she had a little nap.

Then she busied herself, lifting the corn and meal and little loaves to the shelves, hanging her frying-pan on the wall, and putting her kettle and teapot ready on the stove in the corner.

She picked some primrose leaves and sewed them together for a pair of curtains, then she threw wide the door to let the sunshine in.

It fell like an arrow on a dark patch in the wall. It was a couple of cupboards she had missed. She opened the doors, and inside one was a store of honey, left by a family of bees which once lived in the hollow oak. In the other cupboard was a heap of nuts which a Squirrel had once hidden there and forgotten.

She peered at the back of the nut-cupboard and brought out a piece of leather made from a bat's wing. There were little hooks sewn down the side.

"It's a curtain to keep out the draughts," said the Speckledy Hen. She hung it over the doorway, and looped it back for the daytime.

Then, satisfied with her work, she went outside. A little stream ran close by and she filled the kettle. She collected firewood and gathered a few primroses. Then she made a comfortable bed for herself.

"How happy I shall be in my little house!" said she. She laid her first white egg in the nest and sat down to brood over it.

For ten days the Speckledy Hen sat there, and in the nest were ten beautiful eggs. She never went back to the farmyard, for her eggs would have been chilled. Everybody wondered where she was.

"Has anyone seen my Speckledy?" asked the Cock. "She went for a walk and never came back." He kept his eyes open, but although he went quite close to the little house, he never saw the small doorway with the bat's-wing curtain across it.

Little Grey Rabbit wanted to make a cake. She thought of all the spring flowers she would put in it, sweet violets, wood-sorrel, celandines. She wanted one of the Speckledy Hen's famous eggs.

Hedgehog called with the milk and Grey Rabbit ran to the door.

"An extra jugful, please, Hedgehog," said she. "I'm going to make a fine cake. Hare is going to the Speckledy Hen for an egg."

"Haven't you heard?" asked Old Hedgehog solemnly. "She's gone. And her frying-pan and teapot with her."

"Surely not," they all cried.

"Yes. Nobody hasn't seen her for more nor a week."

"I met her going for a walk," said Hare.

"Well, she never came back. And what's more, that there Fox has been about here."

"Oh, darling Speckledy Hen," cried Grey Rabbit in alarm and Squirrel burst into tears. Hare went very pale.

"Don't take on, Miss Squirrel," said Old Hedgehog. "Here wipe your bonny eyes on my handkercher."

He dried her eyes on his big red-spotted handkerchief.

"I don't think the Fox has caught the Speckledy Hen, because she is far too clever for him," said Grey Rabbit.

"She's too cunning for that old Fox," said Hedgehog, nodding his head.

"Perhaps the Hen is hiding from the Fox and can't get home," said Grey Rabbit.

"I'll tell little Fuzzypeg to keep a look-out for her when he goes to school," said Hedgehog.

Now all this time the Speckledy Hen had been sitting on her eggs in her little warm house. She was happy and content. She chuckled as she thought of the day she would lead home a fine brood of chicks.

Through the wet grass walked the Fox, his nose to the earth. He sniffed and he sniffed, and he looked to right and to left, and he came to the little doorway. The curtain was drawn across and he lay down and waited till morning.

"Somebody lives here, and somebody will come out. Then I shall have company for breakfast," said he.

The Speckledy Hen was asleep on her eggs, but she heard the Cuckoo call "Cuckoo! Cuckoo!" and the Blackbird whistle it was time to get up. She drew back the curtains and peeped out. It was a beautiful clear morning.

The Fox walked round to the little doorway, and put his nose inside.

"Good morning, Missus," said he.

"Shoo! Go away, you bad Fox," cried the Hen.

"What bright eyes you have, Missus!" said the Fox.

"Shoo! Be off, you bold bad Fox!" shrieked the Hen.

"Won't you invite me inside?" asked the Fox. He knew very well he couldn't get his body through the little hole.

"Shoo! Off with you," cried the Hen.

"Goodbye, Missus! I must leave you as you won't be friends," said the Fox, and he hid behind the tree. The Hen put on her bonnet and crept to the door. She put out her head and a great mouth snapped at her. Her best bonnet was caught in the Fox's jaws.

"Oh, dear me!" she cried, as she sat down on her eggs
again. "My sweet little bonnet! But it might have been my
silly little head."

There was a pecking and a chirping among the eggs,
then one by one the little chicks came out of their shells.
She gathered them under her wings and sang softly to them.

Fuzzypeg was walking home from school, when he saw a
little bonnet lying on a furze bush. Close to it was a long red
animal, keeping guard. Fuzzypeg scurried away as fast as he
could, with his prickles sticking out fiercely.

"There's a little bonnet hanging on a furze bush, father," said
he, when he got home. "It looked like the Speckledy Hen's."

"Where was it?" asked Old Hedgehog.

"Near the stream in Green Pasture," said Fuzzypeg. "There was a Fox hiding near."

"That Speckledy Hen has thrown her bonnet at him," said Old Hedgehog. "She's always been a daring female."

"I'll go and tell Grey Rabbit," said Fuzzypeg. "She will know what to do."

So off he ran to Grey Rabbit's house, and told them the news.

"I'll go and ask Wise Owl," said Hare.

"Take him a present," said Grey Rabbit.

"Your old musical box," said Squirrel.

So away went Hare into the wood. He tinkled the silver bell that hung from the tree where Wise Owl lived.

"What do you want? Have you brought a present?" asked Owl crossly.

Hare held up the musical box and waved his handkerchief.

"Please, Wise Owl! A Fox sits outside a house where Speckledy Hen lives and waits to gobble her up."

"A fox? I've no love for Tod Fox. I'll help you. Keep your musical box," said the Owl. "Somebody must read a nice story to the Fox. Something exciting so that he won't notice anything else."

The Owl dived into his library and returned with a stout little book which he tossed down to Hare.

"Read it!" said he, and banged his door.

Hare ran home, lollopy, lollopy, wondering who would read to the Fox.

Grey Rabbit and Squirrel turned the pages.

"Who will read it?" they asked, sadly.

"I can't make head nor tail of it," said Old Hedgehog, who had strolled in with Moldy Warp. "What about you Moldy Warp?"

The Mole shook his velvety head and sighed.

"My voice isn't what it use to be and my sight is dim. The Fox wouldn't listen to me."

"I can't read these long words," confessed Grey Rabbit.

"I don't know what these little black letters are," said Squirrel.

"It's a book about animals, I think," added Grey Rabbit.

"My Fuzzypeg can read," said Hedgehog proudly. "He's a scollard."

Little Fuzzypeg was called, and he said he could read the book. Off he went, and all the animals sat on the hillock to watch him.

When he got near the oak tree where the Fox was lying in wait, he called out, "Mister Fox. I go to school now."

"Oh, indeed," said the Fox haughtily.

The Speckledy Hen heard the voices and she peeped out. Around her sat the chicks.

"Mother, when can we go out?" asked the little chicks.

"Bide a wee bit," said she.

"I can read," said Fuzzypeg. "Shall I read you a tale, Mister Fox? It must be very dull for you waiting here."

"It is dull," agreed the Fox. "A good tale would cheer me."

"It's called 'The Fox and the Grapes,'" said Fuzzypeg, opening his book. The Fox kept one eye on the little door, and curled round to listen.

So Fuzzypeg began his story.

"A famished Fox saw some clusters of Rich Black Grapes," said Fuzzypeg.

"Rich Black Grapes," echoed the Fox, and he smacked his lips so loudly that the Speckledy Hen shivered.

"Rich Black Grapes, hanging from a trellised vine," said Fuzzypeg.

"Ah! They would hang there!" cried the Fox. "They don't grow on oak trees. They don't grow on blackberry bushes."

There was a minute's silence, and the Speckledy Hen hurried around, collecting her chicks in a bunch, whispering to them.

"You've never seen a vine," continued the Fox, turning his back on the little house. "I have. Down at the Castle, a trellised vine." He sighed. "Go on, Fuzzypeg. I like to hear a true story."

The Speckledy Hen cautiously looked out again. The Fox was curled up, listening to Fuzzypeg who trembled with excitement.

The Hen crept out, and all the little yellow chicks came after her. The Hen seized her bonnet from the furze bush, and started off towards home.

"Ah!" cried the Fox. "How I wish I had those Rich Black Grapes! How sweet they would be! But go on with your tale, Fuzzypeg."

Fuzzypeg went on, in a voice that shook a little as out of a corner of his eye he saw the Speckledy Hen slip behind the tree, and then walk off with her little tribe of chicks.

"He re-re-resorted to all the tricks to get at them, but he wearied himself in vain, for he could not reach them," said Fuzzypeg, struggling with the long words.

"Jemimay!" said the Fox. "It was just the same with me.
I climbed on the greenhouse roof, and I couldn't get them.
So near, and yet so far, as the saying is."

The Speckledy Hen was walking quickly over the field and
all the chicks followed on tiptoe, their tiny wings outstretched
and they never made a flutter of sound.

Fuzzypeg went on, as loudly as he could.

"At last he turned away, saying – saying –"

"Yes? What did he say? What did he say when he couldn't
get the grapes?" asked the Fox.

The Speckledy Hen was now running at full speed with her chickens scurrying after her to the safety of the farmyard.

"What did he say?" asked the Fox again.

"He said, 'The grapes are sour, and not ripe as I thought,' " said Fuzzypeg.

"So it didn't matter very much?" asked the Fox.

"No. It didn't matter at all," said Fuzzypeg loudly.

The Fox sat thinking about this.

"How did the Fox know they were sour if he hadn't tasted?" said the Fox.

"I 'specks he said it to comfort himself," said Fuzzypeg, wisely.

"I 'specks so too. Thank you for the nice tale," said the Fox. "Who wrote it?"

"Mr Aesop," said Fuzzypeg.

"He was a knowing person," said the Fox. "He knew about us."

"I will give it to you," said Fuzzypeg.

"Thank you, kind Fuzzypeg," said the Fox. "I never had a present in my life."

Fuzzypeg tossed the little book to the Fox and walked away.

The Fox went back to the oak tree and sat close to the door. He called through the doorway.

"Are you all right, Speckledy Hen?"

There was no sound. Not a chirp or a rustle. He put his eye to a crack and peered inside. The room was empty.

Then he saw that the bonnet had gone from the bush near the door.

He galloped over to the farmyard, and there sat the Speckledy Hen with her family and the proud Cock standing near. Around her were Hare, Squirrel, Little Grey Rabbit, Old Hedgehog and Fuzzypeg. They were all laughing and chattering.

The Fox watched them for a minute. He hungrily licked his lips, but the farm dog was on guard. The dinner had gone! He had been outwitted!

"The Speckledy Hen was very thin and scraggy, I'm sure," he told himself. "She wasn't worth eating. I am certain she was a tough fowl, and the chickens too."

He galloped away through the long woods, and over the river to his den in the far valley. Under his arm he carried the little book of Fables.

"I shall look at these pictures when I am hungry," he said. He settled himself in his rocking-chair and spelled out the story of 'The Fox and the Grapes'.

"She was very tough, that Speckledy Hen," said he.

"Three cheers for little Fuzzypeg," cried the Cock when Fuzzypeg finished telling him how he saved the Speckledy Hen.

"Hip, Hip, Hip, Hurrah!" they all cried and the Cock called, "Cockadoodle-doo-doo!" so loudly it rang across the wood to the ears of the Fox in his den.

"It all comes of being a scollard and going to school," said Old Hedgehog.

"Now I will make my cake," said Grey Rabbit. "We will have a feast for the Speckledy Hen and her family, and for brave little Fuzzypeg."

Little Grey Rabbit's Paint-Box

HARE WAS LOLLOPING QUIETLY over a field one fine day when he saw a lady sitting on a little stool in the grass. She was busy with a white book and a black box with something nice within. Hare was most astonished, for it was his favourite meadow. He took shelter behind a crooked hawthorn and watched her.

"What is she doing?" he whispered to the bumble-bees, but they never answered at all, for they were busy too.

The lady went on with her work painting the hills, the end of a barn, the hawthorn and the blue sky above. She saw Mr Hare peeping at her, and, smiling to herself, she drew his long ears and round face in her sketchbook.

After some time she placed the open book on a rock near her; she yawned and stretched herself.

"That's enough," she murmured. "I'll have some lunch while it dries."

She went to the low wall, took some sandwiches from a case, and stayed there, eating her lunch, looking across the valley.

Hare ran quickly over the grass to find out what she had been doing.

"Green-grass-making," said he, and he touched the picture with the tip of his tongue.

"Nasty taste," he grunted. Then he saw himself, a little brown hare with two ears and a bright eye.

"That's me, in the looking-glass," he cried, and he tucked the sketchbook under his arm, and ran very fast.

When the lady came back she could not believe her book had vanished. She hunted everywhere, and at last, puzzled and bewildered, she went away.

"Look what I've found," cried Hare, as he dashed into the little house where Squirrel and Grey Rabbit were sewing.

"What is it? A big toadstool?" asked Squirrel.

"A book?" asked Grey Rabbit.

Hare placed the sketchbook open upon the table, with a proud air.

"Cowslip Meadow and you peeping from behind our tree," said Squirrel, touching it gingerly with her paw.

"Hare, is it really you?" exclaimed Grey Rabbit.

"I watched a lady do it," said Hare, leaping up and down. "I was hiding behind a tree, but she got me and put me here."

"Oh Hare. She didn't hurt you, did she?" asked Grey Rabbit, tenderly.

"No Grey Rabbit. I felt nothing except an ache with keeping still so long. I waited till she moved away. She left this book. People often leave things behind them."

"Yes," agreed Squirrel. "There was that pink hanky Grey Rabbit made into a nightcap."

"And a crooked sixpence Moldy Warp found," added Grey Rabbit. "People leave things behind, bits of paper I stuff down holes, and scraps of bread the birds eat."

"Well, she left this book," continued Hare, turning the pages.

"No writing," said Grey Rabbit. "Only pictures. A pretty book."

"Here's Wise Owl's tree," said Grey Rabbit. "She hasn't seen Wise Owl's bell and his door."

"She doesn't go very near," explained Hare. "She doesn't notice all the leaves and ladybirds and insects."

So they flipped the pages over with their furry paws, and gazed at pictures of fields and trees, with an occasional cottage, and the hills in the distance.

When Milkman Hedgehog came the next day with the cans of milk they invited him indoors and showed him the strange book.

"Aye, it's that lady-artist, staying at the farm," said Old Hedgehog at once. "I knows her by sight. She's always in the fields. She means no harm, but when I tasted some of the paint in her box, all in tidy little flat cakes, I felt very poorly. I was real badly. You didn't eat any, did you, Mr Hare?"

"No, I only took a lick of the picture. The box was shut," said Hare, thankful he had escaped. "I had to hurry off with the book; she left it on a stone."

"You ought not to have took it, Mr Hare," said Hedgehog, gravely. "She left it to dry. I've seen her do that before."

"You must take it back, Hare," said Grey Rabbit.

Hare pouted. "Finding's keeping."

"You can't find if it isn't lost," said Squirrel.

"Yes, I can," cried Hare, quickly. "I find lots of things, snail shells, jay's blue feathers, striped pebbles, green acorns, and none of 'em is lost. This old book isn't lost, it's left."

"Now, take it back, do, Mr Hare," said Old Hedgehog.

"Let me show everybody first," pleaded Hare, and Grey Rabbit agreed.

So Hare ran out to show the pictures to Moldy Warp the Mole.

"They are not as lasting as that Roman picture I once saw deep in the earth," said the Mole. "If you left these out in the rain for a day they would melt away, they would run."

"That was made of stone, a dolphin," answered Hare.

"You and Grey Rabbit could paint if you tried," continued the Mole, rubbing a picture with his little hand.

"How?" asked Hare.

"Oh, you have a brush, and you paint," said Mole, airily. "Very easy."

"A hearth-brush? A sweeping-brush? A besom? A clothes-brush?" cried Hare.

"No, nor a Fox's brush," laughed Moldy Warp. "A thin brush, made of a feather, or hair, or even your own paw, Hare. It's hairy and soft. It would be good for big things like fields."

"Do you really mean it, Moldy Warp?"

Hare leapt on top of the mole-hill and down again.

"Of course you can, Grey Rabbit too, and Squirrel. All artists."

Hare danced away with the sketchbook, singing loudly for all to hear.

"I'm going to be an artist, an artist-fellow; I'm going to paint a picture, red and blue and yellow."

He leaped away to find the Speckledy Hen. There was a picture of her in the book.

"What did you say, Hare? Me? That's not me," cried the flustered Hen. She pecked the sketch of a fat little hen feeding in the farmyard; her sharp beak tore a hole in the paper.

"It's not me," she spluttered, cackling loudly. "It doesn't speak or move. You could paint a better picture yourself, Hare."

"Could I?" asked Hare.

"Take one of my feathers and try," said the Hen and she pulled out a feather and gave it to Hare.

So Hare hurried away delighted, to find little Fuzzypeg.
Fuzzypeg was not impressed. "It's not as nice as my book of
Fables I once read to the Fox. Will you show it to the Fox,
Hare?" he asked.

"No," said Hare, shortly, and then he started, for the Fox was
watching him.

"Let me look," said the Fox sternly, and he stepped leisurely
from the edge of the wood and straightened his red jacket.

"A book?" he continued. "I like books, especially picture
books. Am I in it yet?"

"No," spluttered Hare. "N–n–not yet."

The Fox turned the pages. "Hare and a duck and a fat hen, and some rabbits," he murmured. "A good supper. I'm hungry."

He looked intently at Hare, but Hare took out his watch.

"Not dinner-time yet," said Hare. "Not quite supper-time, either." He shook his watch and they both listened.

"Tick Tack, Tick Tack," said the watch, more loudly than usual and the Fox, who did not like ticking noises, moved away.

"I'm going to be an artist," said Hare, boldly. "So is Grey Rabbit. I will paint a picture of you, Mr Fox."

"I'll give you a bit of my brush," said the Fox, and he pulled out a few red hairs from his tail, tied them together and presented them to Hare.

"Mind you make it like me," said he.

Hare went on his way, very thoughtful now. He showed the book to the Gipsy's horse grazing on the common, for the caravan and horse and Gipsy were all sketched in bright colours.

Duke whinnied with pleasure.

"You can have your picture," said Hare, tearing it out. "You took us to the seaside when we had the sneezes."

"Thank you, kindly," answered Duke. "Pin it in the caravan, Hare. My master's asleep. He will be pleased."

So Hare pinned the picture to a blanket. Then he went on his way to the river where Water Rat was dreamily rowing his boat, singing to himself.

"Hi! Water Rat!" called Hare. "Come here!"

Water Rat tied the little skiff to a reed and swam ashore.

"A book? Is it Wise Owl's?" he asked.

"No. Made by an artist. Pictures in it. Rivers and fields and me," said Hare.

"My river," said Water Rat, as he looked at the scene. "But it is too dry."

He poured a little river water over it.

"It belongs to a lady," Hare told him.

"I remember her," returned Water Rat. "She threw me a sandwich one day."

He stared hard at the picture. Then he broke off a flowering-rush, searched for a patch of reddish mud, and, using the rush as a paint brush, he skillfully sketched a little boat on the river with himself at the oars.

"That's how it should be," said he. "Keep the brush. You and Squirrel and Grey Rabbit can paint with it. Use mud and wood-ash and honey."

"Thank you," said Hare, doubtfully.

"You must show this to Wise Owl. Here's his tree," said the Water Rat.

"I suppose I must," sighed Hare. "I 'specks he'll eat it all."

He went reluctantly to the wood with the damp sketchbook under his arm.

"Tinkle! Tinkle!" rang the little silver bell. There was a shuffle aloft and Hare pulled the bell again.

"Don't ring twice!" hooted the Owl, crossly. "Who's there? Go away whoever you are. Too-whit! Too-whoo!"

"It's me! Hare! I've got a book," called Hare, shakily.

"A book? Is it for me?" Wise Owl came to the door, wide awake with sudden interest.

"It belongs to an artist. There's your tree in it," shouted Hare.

Wise Owl dropped silently down to the tree roots and turned the pages, muttering and mumbling to himself.

"Yes, it's my tree, all right," said he. "No bell, no door, no owl. Not safe."

He tore out the picture, and swallowed it. Then, with the sketchbook in his beak he flew back and disappeared.

"Oh dear!" groaned Hare. "He's going to eat everything. Just as I feared."

Hare waited with a sinking heart.

Suddenly the book fluttered down, and with it a parcel and a feather.

"Take your old book, Hare," hissed Wise Owl. "Here's a paint-box and a brush for Grey Rabbit. Let her try. I've added my picture to the collection."

The brush was made of Wise Owl's breast feathers, soft as a shadow, and the leaf-covered box was tied with looped grass.

Hare hurried home after that, eager to show Wise Owl's presents. He flung the bedraggled book on the table with the small brush and the green box, and he sunk exhausted in the rocking chair.

Squirrel and Grey Rabbit turned the damp pages.

They found the nice little boat painted in river-mud, and the hole the Speckledy Hen had made, and the marks where two pages had been torn out. Then, on a nice clean page they discovered Wise Owl's picture. It was signed with a large O, so they knew it was Wise Owl's picture.

"The full moon," whispered Squirrel.

The beautiful golden moon shone on the page, lighting up the whole room. Around spread the deep blue sky, covering the page.

"He has painted his best friend," murmured Grey Rabbit. "The moon and Wise Owl go together."

Grey Rabbit picked up the soft painting brush, and stroked her cheek with it. Then she opened the green-leaf box.

"Oh! Oh!" she cried. "It's a paint-box for me. It has me on the lid, but of course, you can all use it."

There was a row of little paints inside – blue from the violet, pink from the wild rose, yellow from the cowslip, purple from the grasses, grey from the shadows and black from the night.

"He has made these himself," said Grey Rabbit. "I must take him a present."

"Make him a picture," said Hare.

"I can only paint little earth things, not a moon or stars or sun," replied Grey Rabbit.

Hare took the sketchbook back to the field and placed it carefully on the rock.

"Won't she be surprised when she sees Wise Owl's picture!" said he to himself. "I wish we could have kept it."

He waited behind the tree, nibbling the grass, smelling the scents, until the lady appeared with a friend.

"I left it on that rock," said she. "Oh there's something white! Can it be? Yes, it is. It is my lost book."

She hurried across the grass, and picked it up with cries of astonishment.

"Two pages torn out, and look! A little boat on the river with a water-rat!"

Then she gave a gasp of amazement.

"Here's the moon! It shines! This is pure magic! Who could have done it?"

Hare rolled on the grass with laughter, then went gallumping home to tell the tale.

Squirrel and Grey Rabbit were busy, painting on strips of
silver-birch bark which Squirrel had gathered. Grey Rabbit
used the feather brush of Wise Owl, Squirrel had the flowering
rush, so Hare joined them and painted with Speckledy Hen's
ragged feather and his own soft paw, and the hairy brush from
the Fox.

They worked so hard they forgot to have tea, and they were
still painting when the moon rose in the sky. Wise Owl flew
over: he peered through the window at three small animals;
he tapped at the pane with his beak.

"Too-whit! Too-whee! Any pictures for me?" he called.

So they put down their brushes and showed their work.

Squirrel had painted a dish of cakes, pink cakes and red cakes, cream buns and plum cake, for she thought Wise Owl would enjoy them. They looked as good as real ones.

Grey Rabbit had made a picture of the little house at night, with the candle shining through the window, and Wise Owl flying over the roof.

Hare had painted a picture of the Fox, with his red hair on end and his mouth open, and who should be riding on his back but Hare himself! Hare held a long stick in his paw and he guided Mr Fox with reins.

Squirrel and Grey Rabbit laid their paintings on the grass outside, with a candle, and Wise Owl flew down to inspect them.

"Very good work," said he. "You are artists now.
I will hang these over my bookcase. I shall look
at the little house and know you are safe inside
because the candle is burning. I shall look
at the plate of cakes and I need not go
a-hunting. There's plenty to eat."

He flew back to his tree and hung
the pictures on the wall, but he had to go
hunting after all as Squirrel's cakes were not
good to eat. However, it made him happy
to look at them.

Hare stepped softly through the garden
gate and he stuck his picture to a tree so
that the Fox would find it. He heard a rustle,
and he scampered back as fast as he could go.
When he was safe in the garden he turned
round. There was the Fox staring at his picture
in the moonlight, turning it upside down
and every way.

"Thank you, Hare, artist," cried the Fox. "A good likeness in every direction. I am glad to see you are so anxious to have supper with me that you are riding on my back. Let it be soon! Roast hare and redcurrant jelly!"

Hare didn't wait to explain. He dashed indoors and drew the bolts.

"The Fox didn't understand my picture after all," he told Grey Rabbit.

"Never mind, Hare. We are all artists now, and sometimes real artists aren't understood," said Grey Rabbit, soothing him. "You are a clever Hare and you painted the Fox."

They ate their supper and then they looked out of the window to say "Goodnight" to the moon.

"Goodnight, Moon," they called, bowing their little heads, and a silvery music answered from the heavens.

"Goodnight, small animals. Goodnight."

The Knot
Squirrel Tied

ONE MORNING Rat came to his door and gazed up and down with a weary eye. Then he slowly hobbled out to the hazel spinney and made a crutch to help himself get along.

Mrs Rat shut the door after him.

"Alas!" she sighed. "It hasn't been the same since he stole the food from Grey Rabbit's house, and that impudent Squirrel tied a knot in his tail."

Rat crept along the shadow of the wall. No longer could he scamper with his tail rippling behind him. Now it dragged in the heavy knot which Squirrel had tied to remind him of his wickedness. No longer could he thieve or hunt.

"Every day I get thinner and thinner, I never can get a really good dinner," he moaned.

He thought of this as he sidled along by the wall. At last he reached the farm, and he climbed up the narrow stair into the hen house. He knew the Speckledy Hen had laid an egg, for he had heard her boasting to all the world.

Rat crept to the nests. In one of them lay the big brown egg, which had the golden yolk he loved so much. He tucked it under his body, but when he started downstairs the knot in his tail caught in the doorway, and Rat overbalanced.

At that moment the Speckledy Hen looked up.

"My egg! Oh! My dear egg!" she shrieked.

Rat struggled to get free and dropped the egg.

It rolled down the stairway and spilt on the ground and Rat rushed to safety.

"So near and yet so far," he groaned, as he rubbed his sore shins and rested in a hole in the wall. Then he buckled his belt more tightly and slouched around the corner.

Rat crept into the barn where bags of meal stood in a corner. Here was a lucky find! He gnawed a hole in one sack, and had just started to eat the sweet delicious grain, when in his excitement he moved clumsily, and the knot in his tail thumped on the boards.

Into the barn came the farmyard cat, with her eyes gleaming, and her large mouth wide open.

What a race Rat had for the door!

How his tail thumped behind him! He only just got safely away, with his coat torn.

"That was a near squeak," said he, and sat down to think. "Hedgehog is a kindly soul. I'll have a talk with him at milking time."

He waited all afternoon till Hedgehog came trotting across the field with his milk pails jingling-jangling on the chains.

The Rat watched Hedgehog milk a cow and turn away with the warm milk frothing in his little pails. He licked his lips hungrily and then stepped softly after.

Old Hedgehog heard the thump of the tail, and exclaimed without turning around, "Is that you, Rat? Keep away from my milk pails."

"Mr Hedgehog," said Rat humbly. "A word with you, Sir."

Hedgehog put down the pails and waited.

"I never get anything to eat nowadays," said Rat.

"What do you want me to do, Rat? I'll give you a drink of milk if you like."

The kindly Hedgehog held out a pail and Rat drank it all up with eager gulps.

"Please, kind Hedgehog," whined Rat. "Give me some advice. Everyone knows how wise you are."

"First time I've been called wise," said Old Hedgehog.

"How can I get the knot undone, Hedgehog?" asked Rat.

"Let me see what I can do. My fingers are all thumbs, but I'll use my prickles."

"Oh! Oh! Oh-oo ooh!" squealed Rat as Hedgehog tugged at the knot with his spikes.

"I can't undo it, Rat. Clever fingers fastened it," said he. "Go and ask Mole's advice."

Rat tramped up the field. There was Mole's house, with Mole digging in his garden. He put down his spade.

"Good afternoon, Rat," said he. "May I ask what brings you here?"

"Please, Mole, can you untie the knot in my tail?" asked the Rat in a tiny, sad little voice. "Hedgehog sent me to you, for he couldn't loosen it."

Without a word Mole trotted indoors, and returned with a bowl of soup and a slice of bread.

"Eat this," said he. "Then I will look at it."

Rat thanked him and gobbled up the food.

Then Mole seized the knot with his long pink fingers and struggled and tugged, but still the knot wouldn't come undone.

"It's Squirrel's tying," said he, "but I don't think even her clever fingers could undo this knot. The only one who can help you is Wise Owl."

"I daren't go to him," said Rat.

"Take him a present," replied Mole.

"I am so poor, I have nothing," said Rat to himself as he turned away.

He put his hand in his pocket and brought out a ragged handkerchief and a bone.

"I haven't even a knife, but my teeth are as sharp as a razor. They will do the job."

He sat down on a log and gnawed at the bone. He bit a piece off here, and a slip off there, and a snippet from one end, working away, polishing and rubbing as he went. Night came before he had finished, and he took home his carving.

"Have you bought any food, Rat?" asked his wife, when she opened the door.

"Nothing, wife," said Rat, "but tomorrow I'm going to see Wise Owl." He showed his wife his carving and she sat admiring it.

It was a little white ship with rigging and sails, and tiny portholes. At the prow was a seagull with outstretched wings.

The next day Rat set off with his ship. The billowing sails were nearly transparent with his polishing, and the ropes were like cobwebs.

On the way to Wise Owl's he had to pass Little Grey Rabbit's cottage. Delicious smells came from the window, and Rat crept up to see what was being cooked. He didn't want to get to Owl's house till dusk, so there was plenty of time.

Little Grey Rabbit and Squirrel were making tartlets. Grey Rabbit rolled out the pastry with her little rolling pin, and Squirrel lined the patty pans ready for the raspberry jam.

"Grey Rabbit, Grey Rabbit," called Hare, running up the garden path and bursting into the kitchen.

Rat hid under the juniper bush and Hare passed him without noticing.

"Haymaking has begun!" said he. "Can we all go and play in the hayfield? The grass will be hay tomorrow with this sunshine."

"Oh, let's," cried Grey Rabbit, and she waved her rolling pin excitedly. "We'll invite Mole and Hedgehog and Fuzzypeg to join us, and we'll have tea in the hayfield tomorrow evening."

"I'll make some treacle toffee to take with us," said Hare. He took a saucepan and measured out butter and treacle and sugar. He stirred it over the fire, getting in Squirrel's way, and knocking over the flour bin.

Soon a sweet smell came into the room.

Little Grey Rabbit put her tartlets in the oven, and Hare set his toffee on the windowsill to cool.

Then they all went out in the garden and sat among the flowers, sipping lemonade and fanning themselves with leaves.

Rat crept up to the back door, and looked into the cosy kitchen. He knew his way about.

"Ah!" he sighed, and he dragged his unwilling tail over the doorway. "I'm safe for a few minutes."

He crouched down by the fire, and sniffed the savoury smells of raspberry tartlets which came from the oven. He opened the oven door and poked his nose in the hot jam.

"Oh!" he squeaked in a muffled voice.

"Too hot!"

He dipped the tip of his tail in the cooling toffee, but that was too hot, also. Through the open window he heard the three friends make plans for the picnic.

"There's my chance," said Rat. "I'll come along tomorrow and see what I can find."

He looked again at his little ship, white as ivory, and pretty as a picture. Then he shuffled out of the house, and went through the wood to Wise Owl's house in the great beech tree.

He rang the little silver bell which hung from the door, and the sleepy bird came to see who wanted him in the daylight.

"Rat!" said he gruffly. "What do you want?"

"I've bought you a present, Wise Owl." Rat spoke in a trembling voice.

Wise Owl sat waiting, with his large round eyes staring at the unfortunate rat, while Rat fumbled in his pocket and brought out the little ship.

"Hm-m," said Wise Owl, flying down. "A nice bit of carving. Pity you don't do more work, Rat. Why not try to work instead of to thieve?"

"Please, Wise Owl, will you unknot my tail?" asked Rat humbly. "I am as thin as a leaf, and no one is clever enough to unknot me."

Owl hummed to himself and turned the tiny bone ship over and over.

"I'm afraid you are still a thief, Rat. What about Speckledy Hen's egg? What about the farmer's corn? Where did that jam come from, which I see on your nose? And that treacle toffee on the end of your tail?"

Rat fidgeted uneasily. What keen eyes had Owl!

"The knot will stay tied until you turn over a new leaf, Rat!"

Owl shut his door and went back to his library, holding the little ship in his claws. He took down his book on sailing ships.

"Quite correct in every detail," said he.

Rat hobbled painfully back through the wood, turning all the green leaves he could reach, but still his tail remained knotted. However, he felt happier, for he had made something, and Owl had looked pleased with it.

The next day, as usual, he paid his visit to the farmyard, to see what he could pilfer. He walked up to the hen roost and there was the Speckledy Hen's latest egg. Rat looked at it with longing eyes. Speckledy Hen was a good-natured silly creature. He would leave her egg.

He turned away and started to go down the stair. Was it imagination? He felt a loosening in his tail. The knot thumped less noisily as he slid down.

The Speckledy Hen ran shrieking to her precious egg. There it was, safe and sound! She couldn't understand. Had Rat turned over a new leaf?

Rat went into the barn. There was litter on the floor, and he seized a bunch of twigs. Up and down the stones he went, sweeping softly, with scarcely a glance at the meal bag, until the floor was clean.

Then he went up to the sack and gazed at its bulging sides. A pity to mess up the floor again! There would be raspberry tartlets waiting for him. He turned away, and another little hitch in his tail seemed to be loosened.

He went to Hedgehog's house under the hedge.

"Can I do any little thing for you, Hedgehog?" he asked.

Old Hedgehog stared. "Do you mean a little burglary?" he asked.

"No. I'll help you carry your milk pails to the neighbours," said Rat. "Try me."

So Hedgehog trusted him with the milk for the Red Squirrel.

Rat took the milk to the Red Squirrel's door, and knocked gently. He filled the jug at the foot of the tree, and turned away.

Rat walked through the fields. Both his heart and his tail felt lighter, and when he got back to Hedgehog's house, there was a hunch of bread and cheese waiting for him. Fuzzypeg peeped round the corner. Rat put his hand in his pocket and brought out a dozen oak apples, which he gave to the astonished little hedgehog for marbles.

As evening came there were sounds of gaiety in the hayfield. Squirrel and Little Grey Rabbit in blue sun bonnets were raking the hay, and Hare was piling it up into haycocks.

Hedgehog and Fuzzypeg came to help and tossed it with their prickles. Then Mole joined them, with a little hayfork which he had made.

Rat stood looking at the happy scene – an outsider. He was on his way to Grey Rabbit's house, where he hoped to find the raspberry tartlets waiting for him. He wouldn't be caught this time! He knew his way about, and Squirrel was safe for an hour or two.

Then he noticed the feast spread out under the hedge, not far from him. There it lay, in the shade of the foxgloves, with no one to guard it!

There was a little white cloth and on it a basket filled with raspberry tartlets! So it was of no use to go to the house, for food was here!

There were nut leaves laden with wild strawberries and
raspberries, and a jug full of cream. There was crab apple jelly
and sloe jam, little green lettuces and radishes like rosebuds, and
a big plum cake, and the treacle toffee!

Rat's mouth watered. He stared so hard at the plum cake
that he felt he could taste its delicious sugary crust.

Then he turned away and walked home.

A great pink cloud lay in the sky, and swifts cut across the
blue air. Rat gazed up at the sky, at the birds, so light and free,
and at that moment he felt light and free too. The last knot in
his tail had come undone. He was a happy Rat, loosened from
his fetters, and he ran home to tell his wife whisking his tail
around his head.

"I saw Rat staring at our feast," confided Grey Rabbit to the others as they sat among the foxgloves. "He didn't touch a thing."

"Rat helped to carry my milk today, and swept the barn clean," said Old Hedgehog.

"Rat gave me some marbles," cried Fuzzypeg.

"I wonder if Wise Owl gave him some good advice," mused the Mole.

The next morning Rat came to Little Grey Rabbit's house. He carried a pair of shears and a scythe and he walked with a quick light step.

"Can I gather your firewood, Grey Rabbit?" said he. "Can I mow your lawn, or cut your hedge?"

"Why! The knot has gone from your tail, Rat!" exclaimed Grey Rabbit. "Who untied it, Rat?"

"It came undone by itself," replied Rat modestly.

"I'm not a thief any more. I understand now what Wise Owl meant when he told me to turn over a new leaf. I shall work for my living."

He took up his shears and cut the hedge, making peacocks and balls and ships. He mowed the lawn as smooth as silk, and he pulled up every tiny weed in the garden.

He went in the wood to gather sticks, and as he passed under Owl's tree, the wise bird looked out.

"Ho! Ho!" he hooted. "A reformed Rat. The knot is not! A skillful Rat! An artist! Go on with the good work, Rat, and bring me another present someday. I shall be honoured to accept it."

The Rat blushed through his dusky skin with pride, but he went on gathering sticks. When he had a great bundle he carried it to the door of the little house.

Rat went home with his wages in his pocket, a respectable working animal.

"I'm going to carve something else," said he to his wife. "You've never seen anything like what I'm going to make!" He sat down at the table with his little white bone, and began to carve – but that is a secret for another time!

Wise Owl's Story

Wise Owl lived in the hollow oak tree in the middle of the wood. Anyone could see it was Wise Owl's house, for a little silver bell with an eagle on it hung beside the front door.

There were windows high up in the tree, and a wisp of blue smoke came out of the chimney among the leaves when Owl was at home.

The house was very old and very untidy, and cobwebs hung from the ceiling. There were little attics and storerooms all over the tree, filled with old wood and spiders. Wise Owl never went into these rooms, for he kept to his kitchen, his bedroom and his study.

In the bedroom there was a little four-poster bed, with a small carved owl perched on each bedpost.

In the kitchen was a frying pan, but in the study were all Owl's books of wisdom.

One evening, just as dusk fell, Owl sniffed at the cool air which came through the window.

"A storm's brewing somewhere," said he to himself. "There will be a gale tonight. I must shut the windows before I go out, or my books will get wet."

That night the wind whirled through the wood in a fury. It tossed the trees and snapped the branches. It rattled and banged at the doors and windows of all the little houses in the fields and hedgerows.

Mole, in his underground house knew nothing of the storm, but Mrs Hedgehog awoke her husband in the cottage close by.

"There's a crash!" said she. "Get up, Hedgehog and see what's the matter."

Old Hedgehog crawled sleepily to the window, and stared out. On the ground under the hedge was a little hollow chimney, rolling among the leaves.

"Th' chimbley's come off," said he. "It was a great noise for our little chimbley."

"What shall we do? Suppose the house blows away?" cried Mrs Hedgehog.

"Our house is safe enough, wife. It's the big things that goes in a storm," said Hedgehog, climbing back into bed.

When Wise Owl's hunting was over, he tried to fly back to his tree, but it wasn't there!

"Am I bewitched? Have I come to the wrong wood?" said he. Then he looked down to the ground and he saw the oak tree stretched out like a fallen giant.

The door was broken off, books lay scattered on the grass and the silver bell had gone.

"Too-whit! Too-whoo!" cried the Owl. "What shall I do?"

His great wisdom deserted him, and he was just a lonely, unhappy owl, very wet and very tired, with no home to rest in. The next morning the gale dropped, but the rain poured down.

Little Grey Rabbit could hear the patter of the drops on the roof as she dressed, and she looked from her window at a drenched world.

"I wonder what that crash was I heard in the night," said she to herself. "I'll just slip out while the others are asleep. I want to wear my new galoshes."

She wrapped a cloak over her shoulders and ran out in the wet, down the path to the wood.

"My feet are quite dry!" she exclaimed, as she paddled through a pool.

When she got near Wise Owl's house, she saw the fallen tree and all the tumbled wet books.

"Oh! Poor Wise Owl! What will he do with no home?" she cried.

She looked round for Wise Owl, but he was nowhere to be seen, so she hurried back with her sad news.

"We must all do something," said Hare, as he ate his porridge.

"Yes, something really useful," said Squirrel.

"Should we invite him here as our guest till he finds another house?" asked Grey Rabbit.

"Here?" exclaimed Hare. "In this house, Grey Rabbit? Are you mad?"

"He'd break our cups with his wings," said Squirrel. "He'd be asleep all day, when we wanted to make the beds. Besides, his ways are not our ways." She shivered.

"No, it wouldn't do," agreed Grey Rabbit. "He must have a house of his own. A nice big house to hold all those books of wisdom which I saw lying in the rain."

There was silence for a moment, and then Grey Rabbit said, "Suppose we go out and look for one for him? We will wait till the rain stops, and then we will take sandwiches and spend the day house-hunting."

"Sandwiches? Splendid!" cried Hare. "I love house-hunting!" He ran to the door and looked out.

"There's a rainbow in the sky, Grey Rabbit. We can go quite soon."

The three animals set out on their expedition through the wood, but although they looked to the right and the left, high up and low down, they couldn't find a hollow tree.

They took their sandwiches out of their pockets and sat down to eat them near Owl's fallen tree.

Grey Rabbit fished a little dictionary out of the pool and wiped it on her handkerchief. Squirrel found a book of nursery songs in a briar bush. Hare picked up a history book, but that was quite dry.

"I wonder where Wise Owl is," said Grey Rabbit, and she peeped through the door into the dusty rooms.

"Let us all go different ways," said Squirrel. "Then if we haven't found a house by teatime, we will go home."

Hare set off down an inviting little path and soon found himself out of the wood, in a wet green meadow. There in the grass grew round, white satiny knobs.

"Mushrooms!" he cried, and he filled his pockets. He forgot all about Wise Owl's house. At the gate he met an elderly rabbit, and gave him a pawful of mushrooms, and then ran across the fields.

Squirrel started off along a little path in the opposite direction, and came to a mountain ash tree.

Up she ran, and rubbed her cheeks against the scarlet berries. She picked a bunch, and threaded them on a grass. Then she hung them round her neck. She too forgot all about Wise Owl and his home, as she lay curled up high in the air.

Little Grey Rabbit ran along the path to the west, looking to right and left for a hollow tree. She dodged in and out, sniffing and searching.

She worked so hard she did not notice that the afternoon had passed, and evening was approaching. She tapped each tree, and marked them, moving farther and farther from home, until at last she heard the sound she had been listening for all day.

She stopped in front of a great beech tree and tapped again. It was hollow!

Here was a house for Wise Owl! Little Grey Rabbit ran round the trunk and pulled away the brambles and leaves which concealed the opening. Then she went inside.

There was a splendid empty house!

It was rather damp, but a little fire would soon dry it. There were three rooms, and lots of attics, and shelves all round the walls.

She went to the door and looked out. The moon was rising behind the hill, and a soft golden glow spread over the wood. Grey Rabbit thought of her home, and the supper table and bright fire, and she felt very lonely. She didn't know where she was, and there was nothing to be done, except to stay there all night.

She picked up a tiny glow-worm and carried it in with her. She climbed onto a rough shelf and fell asleep, with the glow-worm shining like a little night-light.

When Hare went home, he found Squirrel sitting rocking herself backwards and forwards.

"Where is Little Grey Rabbit?" asked Hare.

"She probably met Wise Owl, and they talked about tails and bells and hollow trees," said Squirrel.

They had tea without her, but when suppertime came, and there was no Little Grey Rabbit, they both grew anxious.

Hare put a lighted candle in the window and called, "Coo-ee. Coo-ee."

Wise Owl came out of the woodshed. "Did you call?" he asked coolly.

"We've lost Grey Rabbit," explained Hare.

"She is looking for a house for you."

"A house for me?" echoed Wise Owl. "I am going to live in your woodshed."

Then he stepped into the house and snapped up all the mushrooms and hot buttered toast which lay ready for supper.

"I'd better go off and find Grey Rabbit," said Wise Owl. "You stay here, and wait up for her."

Hare mopped his brow. "Whew!" he cried.

"I never thought I should live to see the day when an Owl would come into the kitchen and eat my supper before my very eyes!"

Wise Owl flew over the woods, calling, but either the tree was too thick or Grey Rabbit was too fast asleep, she never heard his voice, and he had to return without her.

Hare and Squirrel were very much alarmed.

"I am going to sleep now," said Wise Owl. "Don't disturb me. You two must go out and look for her. The morning's here, and Hedgehog the milkman is starting on his rounds. Off you go!"

"He orders us about as if he lived here," complained Squirrel. "Oh, I do wish Grey Rabbit would come back!"

There was a sound outside, the door was pushed open, and in came Little Grey Rabbit, looking as fresh as a daisy. She had washed in a stream and brushed her hair with a teasel brush.

"Wherever have you been?" cried Hare. "We were just going to look for you. Owl was hunting for you all night."

Little Grey Rabbit turned pale.

"To find you, not to eat you," said Hare crossly.

"I got lost," said Little Grey Rabbit. "But I found a home for Owl!"

"Thank goodness," exclaimed Hare. "Is it a nice house, Grey Rabbit? Owl is in the woodshed, and he won't go away unless it is a nicer house than ours."

"Couldn't we spring-clean it for him, while he is asleep, and put his books inside, and then he will want to go?" asked Squirrel.

"Oh yes!" cried Grey Rabbit.

Then they took buckets and mops and scrubbing brushes and soap, and walked off to the wood.

Grey Rabbit led them to a beautiful beech tree, with golden leaves spreading in a tent overhead.

"It's a fine tree," said Hare, "but where is the door?"
Grey Rabbit pointed out the small hole near the ground.

"Owl won't want to fly down to the earth when he comes home," objected Hare. "Excuse me. I must run home." And away he went.

Squirrel and Grey Rabbit scrubbed and mopped. They washed the little shelves and bookcases, and the cupboards which hung all round the tree.

"Owl will be able to keep all of his books here," said Squirrel, and she put some pointed chestnut leaves on the floor for green carpets. "There's a place for his pen and ink, and—"

"Tape measure and thimble," interrupted Hare, coming in carrying a saw.

"What's that for?" asked Squirrel.

"Do you imagine that Wise Owl would live here with that door? Why, he couldn't get through it without crawling! I'm going to make a door, high up, so that he can fly in!"

He climbed up the steep stairs, and cut a neat door in the tree. Then he cut a window in Owl's study, which was very dark.

"A nice airy house with every modern convenience," said he proudly, as he stepped backwards to view his work, but he trod on the soap and fell downstairs to the bottom of the tree.

"Never leave soap on the stairs, Squirrel!" cried Hare, rubbing his head. So Squirrel placed it on the larder shelf.

The three animals went to the oak tree and collected the books, which were now dry with the wind and the sun. They carried them across to the new house, and arranged them on the shelves.

They returned with Owl's chair, his feather bed and frying pan. Little Grey Rabbit found his nightcap dangling in the nettles. But nowhere could they see the little silver bell.

The house was finished and they stood in the grass admiring it when Hedgehog walked up.

"Hello!" said he. "I've just found Owl's bell. I was walking along the path through the wood, when I heard a tinkly tinkle, and there was a mouse playing with Owl's bell!"

"A bold mouse!" said Hare.

Little Grey Rabbit took the silver bell and polished it.

Then Squirrel ran up the tree and hung it at the side of Owl's front door, and the four walked back to the little house at the edge of the wood.

"Wake up, Wise Owl," they cried. "There's a new house for you in the wood."

"Don't want a new house," muttered Wise Owl sleepily.

"Your books are on the shelves," said Hare.

"Your bell's a-tinkling by the front door," said Hedgehog.

Wise Owl came out and blinked at them.

"Did you say you had put up my tree again?" he asked.

"No. We've found another, a better one," said Little Grey Rabbit.

Without a word Wise Owl flew off.

When Owl saw the silver bell, he pushed open the door.
He walked upstairs, one step at a time, and he looked in all the
cupboards and on the shelves.

"I must give a present each to the Squirrel, the Hare and the
Little Grey Rabbit. They've certainly done me a good turn."

He searched in his treasure box, which was buried deep in
the brown leaf-mould of the wood, and he took them:

A tiny basket carved out of a cherry stone, a sailing boat
made from half a walnut shell, and a little beech tree growing
out of a beech nut!

Now can you guess which had which?

Little Grey Rabbit's
Birthday

Squirrel and Hare were gardening one fine day. "It's Little Grey Rabbit's birthday on Midsummer Day," said Squirrel. "We must give her a nice present."

"A very nice present," agreed Hare. "A cake or something. Something we can all share."

"Yes, a birthday cake with candles on it," said Squirrel.

"I don't like the taste of candles," objected Hare.

"They're not to eat!" cried Squirrel. "They are to show how old you are. Three candles if you are three years old."

"And a hundred if you are a hundred years old," said Hare. "Oh, Squirrel, can we make the cake ourselves?"

"I think so," nodded Squirrel. "But it must be a secret."

Just then Grey Rabbit came running out of the house.

"Grey Rabbit," said Hare. "Squirrel and I have been saying that it will be your b-b—"

"Shh! Not a word!" whispered Squirrel.

"No! It's a secret," said Hare hastily.

"A secret from me?" asked Grey Rabbit.

"It's something that mustn't be told," said Hare with importance.

"You are a funny pair," laughed Grey Rabbit.

"Will you come for a walk to visit the Speckledy Hen? I want some eggs for tea."

"We'll come, won't we Hare?" said Squirrel, throwing down the rake.

They went through the field where Moldy Warp lived.

"Hello!" he cried when the three friends arrived. "This is a surprise." He hurried to fetch glasses of heather ale and brought them outside.

"I'm going to tell," Hare suddenly exclaimed. "I can't keep the secret in. I shall burst!"

"No! No!" cried Squirrel, shaking his arm.

"Come inside, and whisper it to me and the doorpost," said Mole kindly. Hare followed him into the passage.

"It's Grey Rabbit's birthday on Midsummer Day, and we are going to make a cake," he said breathlessly.

"Ah! That is a good secret!" agreed Mole. "I'll give her a present."

"And come to tea with us," said Hare.

"Thank you, Hare," said Mole.

The three friends said goodbye and Grey Rabbit led the way through the wood to the great tree where Owl lived.

Squirrel ran up the tree and called softly through the open window.

"Wise Owl! It's Grey Rabbit's birthday on Midsummer Day."

"Gr-gr-gr," snored Wise Owl, but he heard in his dreams all the same.

They passed into the fields where Hedgehog was coming back from milking.

"Can we have a drink?" asked Squirrel, dancing up to him. "It's thirsty work keeping secrets."

Hare took Old Hedgehog aside and whispered, "It's Grey Rabbit's birthday on Midsummer Day. We are going to make her a cake, and you can come and taste it."

"Ah! Thank ye!" cried Hedgehog.

"Come along, Hare. We shall never get to the Speckledy Hen's house," called Grey Rabbit, "if you spend all the time telling secrets."

When they arrived at the farm, there was the Speckledy Hen walking about.

"We've come for some eggs, Speckledy Hen," said Grey Rabbit.

While the Hen was filling up the basket, Hare whispered in her ear.

"It's Grey Rabbit's birthday on Midsummer Day. We are going to make a cake, and you can come and taste it."

"I'll bring a present for dear Grey Rabbit," whispered Hen.

The next day Squirrel and Hare decided to make the cake.

"We must do it secretly," said Hare. "Won't Grey Rabbit be surprised! She doesn't know we can make cakes."

"We don't know either," muttered Squirrel.

"Grey Rabbit! Go away!" commanded Hare, when Little Grey Rabbit came in from the garden.

"Oh Hare! What have I done? What's the matter?" Her ears drooped and a tear came into her eye.

Squirrel stamped her foot. "Hare! How stupid you are!" she exclaimed. She wiped Grey Rabbit's eyes, and said kindly, "Grey Rabbit! Please will you take a bottle of primrose wine to Wise Owl? He was hooting last night. Moldy Warp would like a visit, and I am sure Fuzzypeg would love to hear a story."

"Then I'll run off at once," said Grey Rabbit, smiling at her two friends.

"Goodbye!" called Squirrel and Hare, and they waved their paws as Grey Rabbit went along the lane.

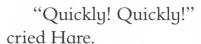

"Quickly! Quickly!" cried Hare.

Squirrel sniffed at all the jars of spices and herbs on the dresser.

"Here's tansy and woodruff, and preserved violets and bottled cherries," she said.

"Here's poppyseed and acorns and beech nuts," said Hare. "Oh, here's the pepper pot. How much shall I put in?"

"A fistful of everything makes a nice cake," said Squirrel.

So they dipped their paws into every jar, and mixed the seeds and herbs in the yellow bowl.

"Is the oven hot?" said a deep voice. There at the window was Old Hedgehog watching them with twinkling eyes.

"I comed with extra milk for the cake," said he. "You didn't ought to put pepper in it."

Hare blushed and tried to hide the pepper pot.

"Oh Hare! We shall have to begin all over again," said Squirrel.

"I'll come and lend a hand," said Old Hedgehog.

He made up the fire and showed Squirrel how to mix the sugar and butter together and how to sprinkle in the currants and spices.

Hare ran to the garden and brought in rose petals and violets – all the sweet-smelling things he could find to add to the cake. He beat up the eggs till they were a yellow froth, and Hedgehog dropped them into the mixture.

"Now I must be off," said Hedgehog. "Remember not to open the oven door till the good rich smell comes out."

They popped the cake in the hot oven and shut the door.

After a while there came a strong sweet smell.

"The cake!" Hare cried. "It's telling us it's ready to come out."

So Squirrel wrapped a cloth round her paw and lifted out the good-smelling cake, as brown as a berry, all puffed up and crinkly with sugar and spices.

They carried it into the garden and hid it under an empty beehive.

The next day when Grey Rabbit had gone out to gather wool from the hedges, Squirrel ran to the garden for the cake. She iced it and wrote:

Grey Rabbit's Birthday

on the top in the pollen dust.

Hare put lots of candles round the edge – big candles, little candles, red and blue and green ones – and then they danced for joy. "It is fit for a fairy queen," they told each other.

They hid the cake in the beehive again, ready for Midsummer Day.

"I'm going to make a fan for Grey Rabbit," said Squirrel. "I shall ask the green woodpecker and the goldfinch for some feathers."

"And I will make a purse for her," said Hare.

Squirrel begged a few feathers from the birds. She put them together, and there was the prettiest little fan of green and gold.

Hare went to the pasture for a puff-ball. He washed the little bag in the dew, then he tied it with ribbon-grasses.

Darkness came and the three little animals went upstairs to bed.

In the night Grey Rabbit was wakened by a faint noise under her window. She slipped out of bed, and putting her cloak over her nightgown, ran downstairs and into the garden.

There, crouched in a sad, prickly little ball, was Fuzzypeg.

"What's the matter, Fuzzypeg?" whispered Grey Rabbit.

"I comed to say Happy Birthday," said Fuzzypeg. "I got out of the window, and I runned very fast, but I heard Wise Owl hooting, and I got frightened."

"Poor little Fuzzypeg," said Grey Rabbit softly. "You had better come into my bed."

She took his paw and led him upstairs.

"I knew you'd take care of me, Grey Rabbit. Happy Birthday."

"It isn't my birthday till tomorrow, Fuzzypeg," said Grey Rabbit.

She tucked him up, then she wrapped her cloak round herself and crept under the bed. She couldn't sleep with a bundle of prickles by her side.

The next morning Hare and Squirrel raced downstairs to get the breakfast.

"I'm going to say Happy Birthday to Grey Rabbit," said Hare.

"So am I," said Squirrel.

"I shall say it first because I'm bigger than you," said Hare.

"No, I shall say it first because I'm the little one," said Squirrel.

They stared at each other crossly.

"Let's both say it together," said Squirrel.

So upstairs they bundled, and they flung open the bedroom door.

"Happy Birthday!" came squeaking from the bed, and out of the blankets came Fuzzypeg's dark head.

"I said it first!" said he.

The noise wakened Grey Rabbit, and she crawled out from under the bed.

Hare and Squirrel were so surprised, they never said Happy Birthday at all. They just stared and stared.

"Milk-o!" the call came from the kitchen. "Has anyone seen our Fuzzypeg? He runned away in the night, and it's my belief he came to see Miss Grey Rabbit."

"Here he is, Hedgehog!" they shouted, running downstairs.

"I said it first," boasted Fuzzypeg. "I said Happy Birthday before any of you."

"He said he would be the first and he's done it," said Old Hedgehog proudly.

"Let him stay for breakfast," pleaded Grey Rabbit, and Hedgehog agreed.

Soon they all sat round the table and ate the nice food.

"It's your birthday, Grey Rabbit," said Squirrel. "So you shall have a holiday. We'll wash up the cups and plates."

"Then I'll go into the garden with Fuzzypeg and show him the flowers," said Grey Rabbit.

When they came to the beehive a stream of honeybees flew out.

"Hare! Squirrel! A swarm of bees is living in our empty hive," called Grey Rabbit. "Isn't it exciting? Listen, they are humming something." This is what they heard:

> *It's Grey Rabbit's Birthday,*
> *She doesn't want money*
> *Or fine clothes or riches.*
> *We'll make her some honey.*

Hare and Squirrel looked at one another and sighed. "Honey out of our cake," they whispered.

At four o'clock Squirrel and Hare sent Grey Rabbit upstairs, while they got ready the tea. Then they ran down the garden to the beehive.

They lifted up the straw skep, and there was the cake, looking nicer than ever. Around it were little pots of honey, each as big as a thimble.

They carried the treasures indoors and placed them on the table. Grey Rabbit came running downstairs.

What a surprise! The table was beautiful with the birthday cake and all the candles alight upon it. The tiny pots of honey shone like gold, and there were dishes of cresses and nuts and cream.

"Oh! Oh!" cried Grey Rabbit. "What's this?"

"It's somebody's birthday cake," said Squirrel.

"It's everybody's cake, and here they come to the feast," said Hare.

Up the path came many little feet. Then there was a rat–tat–tat at the door.

"Come in! Come in!" cried Squirrel.

In trooped Moldy Warp, the Hedgehog family, the Speckledy Hen and a crowd of little animals.

"Many Happy Returns, Grey Rabbit," they cried. They saw the table, the lighted cake and the honey pots.

Then Squirrel gave Grey Rabbit the little fan made of feathers and Hare brought out the purse tied with green ribbon–grass.

Everybody had brought a present, but Moldy Warp's present was the best of all. It was the song of the nightingale in a tiny musical box.

They were all listening to the music, when the door was pushed open and a pair of large blinking eyes appeared.

"I won't come in," hooted Wise Owl, "but I have brought a small token of my regard for Grey Rabbit."

He thrust one claw forward and dropped a book on the table. Then he drifted away as silently as he had come.

"Whew!" exclaimed Moldy Warp. "That was a shock."

"What has he brought?" asked Hare.

"It's called *Wise Owl's Guide to Knowledge*," said Grey Rabbit, holding the tiny green volume.

"Cut the cake, Grey Rabbit!" called Hare. "I'm hungry. Cut the cake!"

So Grey Rabbit cut the beautiful birthday cake and they all had a piece. It was as nice as it looked. Really, Hare and Squirrel had made it very well!

Moldy Warp drank Grey Rabbit's health, Squirrel recited a little poem, and Hare played a tune on his flute.

They all laughed and sang and danced till night came, and then they went home by the light of the moon.

"What a lovely birthday it has been," said Grey Rabbit. "How kind everybody is to me!"

She looked at all the little treasures the woodland folk had brought.

Then she went upstairs to bed, with the musical box under her arm. She turned the handle and the voice of the nightingale came trilling out. From the woods another nightingale answered.

"A Happy Birthday, Grey Rabbit," it seemed to say. "Thank you for all the fun you give us."

A TEMPLAR BOOK

First published in the UK in 2016 by Templar Publishing,
part of the Bonnier Publishing Group,
The Plaza, 535 King's Road, London, SW10 0SZ
www.templarco.co.uk
www.bonnierpublishing.com

Moldy Warp the Mole:
Original edition published in the UK
in 1940 by William Collins Sons & Co

The Speckledy Hen:
Original edition published in the UK
in 1945 by William Collins Sons & Co

Little Grey Rabbit's Paint-Box:
Original edition published in the UK
in 1958 by William Collins Sons & Co

The Knot Squirrel Tied:
Original edition published in the UK
in 1937 by William Collins Sons & Co

Wise Owl's Story:
Original edition published in the UK
in 1935 by William Collins Sons & Co

Little Grey Rabbit's Birthday:
Original edition published in the UK
in 1944 by William Collins Sons & Co

Text copyright © 2016 by the Alison Uttley Literary Property Trust
Illustrations copyright © 2016 by the Estate of Margaret Tempest
Design copyright © 2016 by Templar Publishing
Leaves and snowflake vector shapes designed by Freepik.com

1 3 5 7 9 10 8 6 4 2

ISBN 978-1-78370-488-0

Designed by Nathalie Eyraud
Edited by Susan Dickinson and Ruth Symons

Printed in China